THIS BOOK WAS MADE ESPECIALLY FOR:

Johan

Given with love from:

*D*earest Johan, may each day's blessings shine upon you like the sun upon the water.

$\mathcal{M}$ay each dawn
bring the hope
of the spring crocus . . .

. . . the sweetness of the summer berry . . .

. . . the richness of the autumn harvest . . .

. . . and the magical wonder of winter's warmth.

May you soar like
the robin through
life's sunny days . . .

. . . run like the deer through its shady forests . . .

. . . bend like the willow
when its winds blow . . .

. . . and always have the strength of the ancient oak, who knows that no storm lasts forever.

*M*ay all of nature remind you what a joy you are to the world!

The birds that sing for you . . .

. . . the frogs that
jump for you . . .

. . . the bees that dance for you . . .

. . . and the river that roars with delight
at the very mention of your name.

For you, Johan, are all that is good, all that is bright, all that is beautiful in this world of ours.

$\mathcal{A}$nd that makes you special, indeed.

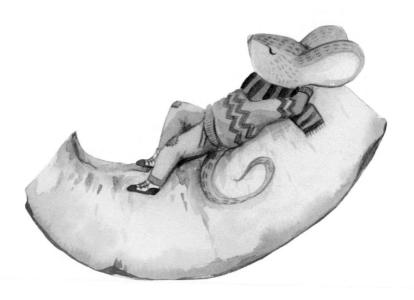

Made in the USA
Las Vegas, NV
22 December 2024

15269257R00021